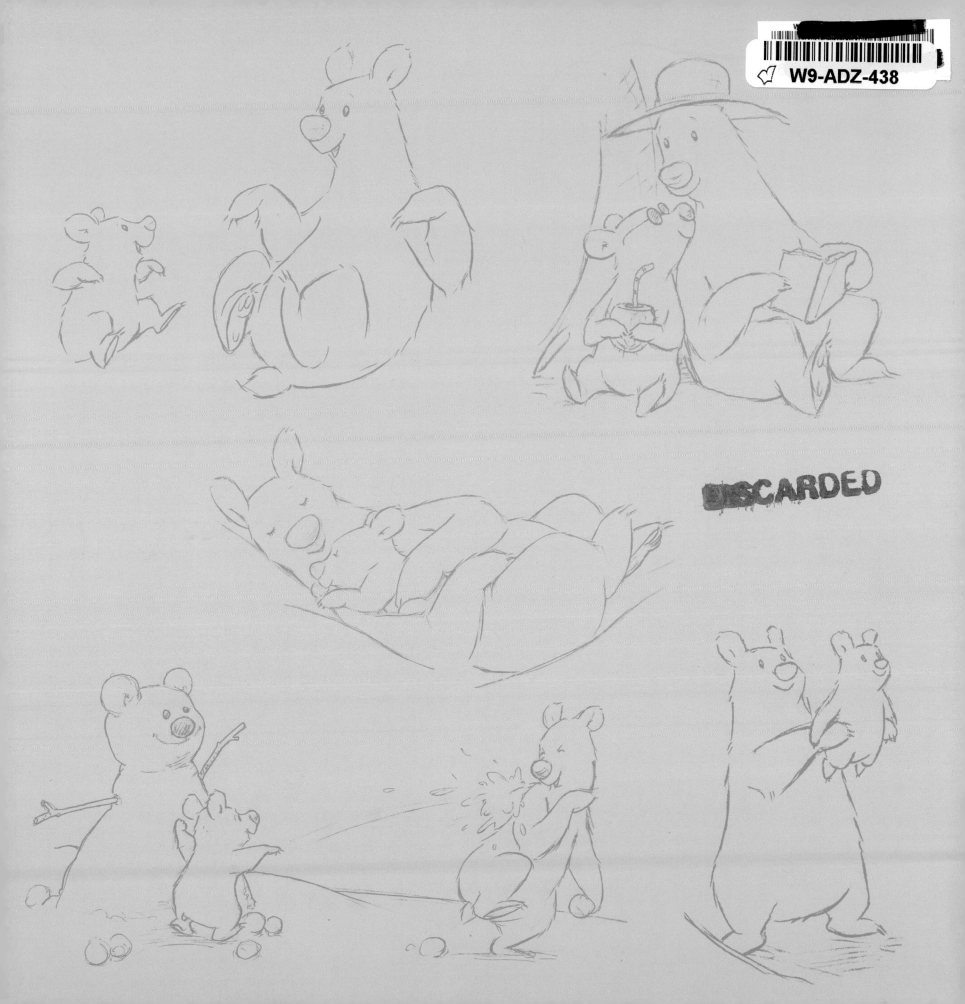

For Anita, with thanks —C.F.

Visit us on the Web! rhcbooks.com

Educators and librarians, for a variety of teaching tools, visit us at RHTeachersLibrarians.com

Library of Congress Cataloging-in-Publication Data
Names: Fuge, Charles, author, illustrator.
Title: Together / Charles Fuge.
Description: First American edition. | New York : Doubleday Books for Young Readers, [2020] | "Originally published in the United Kingdom by Hodder Children's Books, an imprint of Hachette Children's Group, part of Hodder and Stoughton, London, in 2020." | Audience: Ages 0–4. | Summary: Whether stargazing, playing, or cuddling before bedtime, a polar bear parent assures a child that they will never be lonely, because they are together forever.
Identifiers: LCCN 2020010739 (print) | LCCN 2020010740 (ebook)
ISBN 978-0-593-30388-7 (hardcover) | ISBN 978-0-593-30389-4 (ebook)
Subjects: CYAC: Stories in rhyme. | Parent and child—Fiction. | Polar bear—Fiction. | Bears—Fiction.
Classification: LCC PZ8.3.F955 Tog 2020 (print) | LCC PZ8.3.F955 (ebook) | DDC [E]—dc23

MANUFACTURED IN CHINA
10 9 8 7 6 5 4 3 2 1
First American Edition

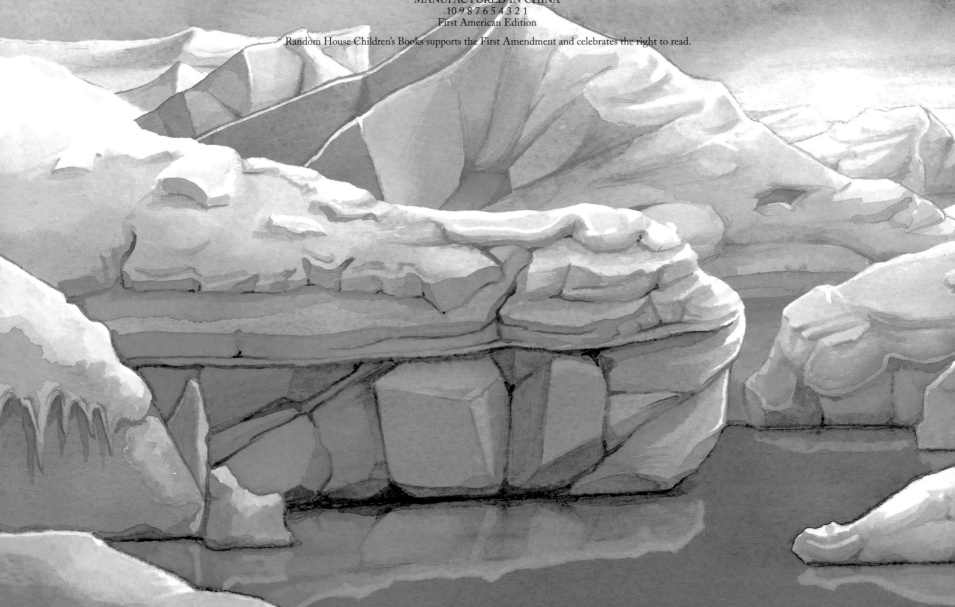

Together

Charles Fuge

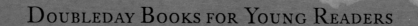

DOUBLEDAY BOOKS FOR YOUNG READERS

As you look at the world
from the safety of home,
though the sky is so vast,
you won't feel alone.

Though the snow seems to go on
forever and **ever**,

you'll never be lonely. . .

because we're together.

Together we **wander**
and **wonder** at things…

and we **fly** through the air,

though we haven't got **wings**.

And when we're together, we don't mind the cold.

We always have each other's warm hand to hold!

We often imagine faraway lands, with parrots and palm trees and warm golden sands.

But then we agree that we **don't need** that stuff....

Just being together is
more than enough!

Sometimes at night, we gaze at the stars,
and we talk about Pluto and Venus and Mars.
You learn new things fast, because you're SO clever....

And learning's such fun

when we are together!

Together we **stand**,

together we . . . **fall.**

Together we travel, one **big** and one small.

Together we laugh and we sing and we

play...

enjoying togetherness every day.

And when you feel worried, and you ask me whether

I might ever leave you, I always say,

"NEVER!"

"Together!" you say, as we cuddle up tight.

"Forever," I whisper, and kiss you goodnight.